Dedicated to my Lisette!
She is the light of my life, full of adventure and happiness.
May all your dreams come true!

"Lissettes Song"

Can you hear me calling, can you hear my song?
I have been waiting my whole life, for you to come along.
This night might be chilly, but with you I won't be cold.
Because I'll stay close to you forever until we both grow old.
You will get all my attention, come rain or shine,
I'll take care of you forever for I am yours, and you are mine.

Hi, how are you?
My name is Lisette, you can just call me Lizzy, guess what? I'm going on a magical, daring and full of adventure quest. A quest to find a unicorn!!!!

Yes, a unicorn, they are real, it's true, a wizard told me, today I am going to find one.

We all know, unicorns can heal and mend, make dreams come true. Did you know, once you make a friend with a unicorn, they are your friends for life. Together you will have a super mega mind connection, where they know what you're thinking
and feeling! Wow huh?

SUPPLIES

- GLOVES (if it gets cold.)
- COAT
- COTTON CANDY — It's there favorite treat.
- CARROTS — because you must eat something healthy.
- MY MAGICAL GOGGLES THAT HELP ME SEE UNICORNS.
- MY MAGICAL UKULELE to sing to them ★ UNICORNS LOVE MUSIC!

I can't wait to find my unicorn.
Ok, now to check my supplies.

The forest needs to be thick with pines. The smell of pine is so pretty, and soothing.

Birds sing their songs all day, and there are tons of beautiful wildflowers.

Can you hear me calling, can you hear my song? I have been waiting my whole life, for you to come along. This night might be chilly, but with you I won't be cold. I'll stay close to you forever until we both grow old.

You will get all my attention, come rain or shine, I'll take care of you forever for I am yours, and you are mine.

I put my ukulele down. I cross my fingers and toes. I tried to cross my eyes, but I just saw two of my nose. It made me feel dizzy. I decide to close my eyes and wait....

I wait, and wait, it felt like hours, maybe even days. I don't know for sure, I lost track of time. I was gazing up at the clouds and seeing all kinds of funny shapes and animals. One even looked like a Dragon eating an ice cream cone.

Suddenly I feel a breeze on my face, a burst of illuminating sunshine flows threw the trees, and I see the most beautiful unicorn.

The Unicorn is so pure, and white, with a silver glittery horn. Her hooves are black as coal, with eyes as green as an emerald ocean. She comes closer to me, and after looking into my eyes, she smiles and touches her forehead to mine.

She kneels on the ground, and allows me to jump on her back. She neighs softly, and immediately starts running through the forest.

We are going so fast it feels like we are flying, I look down, we are!!

She jumps in a loop, I hold tightly to her main, my stomach is full of butterflies. I can't control my laughter, it explodes as the air rushes through my hair, soon we are at the edge of the ocean.

She snuggles me in bed. Even though, it's early morning I know I will have amazing dreams.

Hazel flys home as fast as the light creeps into my room, but I know she will never be far, because she is now my unicorn, and my best friend.

Made in the USA
Middletown, DE
21 November 2022